Cellular

Cellular

Ellen Schwartz

orca soundings

ORCA BOOK PUBLISHERS

Library and Archives Canada Cataloguing in Publication

Schwartz, Ellen, 1949-
Cellular / written by Ellen Schwartz.
(Orca soundings)

Issued also in an electronic format.
ISBN 978-1-55469-297-2 (bound).--ISBN 978-1-55469-296-5 (pbk.)

I. Title. II. Series: Orca soundings
PS8587.C578C44 2010   JC813'.54   C2010-903602-6

First published in the United States, 2010
Library of Congress Control Number: 2010929063

Summary: When Brendan is diagnosed with leukemia, his life
is turned upside down. With a smothering family and distant friends,
all seems hopeless until he meets Lark, terminally ill yet full of life.

Mixed Sources
Cert no. SW-COC-001271
© 1996 FSC
FSC

*Orca Book Publishers is dedicated to preserving the environment and has printed
this book on paper certified by the Forest Stewardship Council.*

Orca Book Publishers gratefully acknowledges the support for its publishing
programs provided by the following agencies: the Government of Canada
through the Canada Book Fund and the Canada Council for the Arts,
and the Province of British Columbia through the BC Arts Council
and the Book Publishing Tax Credit.

Cover design by Teresa Bubela
Cover photography by Masterfile

ORCA BOOK PUBLISHERS
PO Box 5626, Stn. B
Victoria, BC Canada
V8R 6S4

ORCA BOOK PUBLISHERS
PO Box 468
CUSTER, WA USA
98240-0468

www.orcabook.com
Printed and bound in Canada.

13 12 11 10 • 4 3 2 1

For Uncle Gerald

Chapter One

I'm sitting across the desk from Dr. Wong. My mom is beside me, clutching her purse.

Dr. Wong folds his hands. Clears his throat. Glances at the folder in front of him, then at me.

"I'm afraid I have bad news, Brendan. It's leukemia."

It goes right by me. I don't even hear it. I'm so prepared to hear anything else— a virus, mono, meningitis, even avian flu—that it's only when my mom gasps that my mind backs up, rewinds the tape, and I actually hear what he just said.

Leukemia.

I'm going to die.

It can't be.

It must be someone else.

Will it hurt?

Leukemia is for pathetic-looking bald kids with big eyes. Not me.

Is there treatment? Is there a cure?

I'm going to die.

It was a complete shock—but then, looking back, I realized that I should have had a clue. I'd been feeling like crap for months but kept brushing it off.

I had no energy. Got the chills out of nowhere.

Must be the flu.

Had no appetite. Started losing weight.

Must be a stomach thing.

Got pains in my joints. Weird bruises appeared.

Must've worked out too hard at basketball practice. Pulled some muscles. Bumped into guys too hard in the paint.

I knew I should see a doctor, but there was no way I was going to miss basketball. When my mom pestered me, I said I'd go, but *after* the season, *after* I'd led my team to the finals. Only, of course, my scoring dropped off, my stamina disappeared, and Coach, looking puzzled and just a little pissed off, started sitting me on the bench. And, as it turned out, I was nowhere near a basketball court by the time my team played—and won—the finals.

It was only when I couldn't get it up with Cassie that I really began to think something might be wrong. Ah, Cassie. Cassandra Villanueva. Big brown eyes, wavy black hair, luscious mouth.

We started going out when she came on to me at a party. It was early winter. I'd just been named captain of the basketball team. Later I wondered if that had anything to do with it. Cassie had a reputation for going out with all the captains—she'd already gone through football and soccer.

But at that moment who cared if that was why Cassie was after me? Not me. She came into the kitchen, where I was hanging out with Kesh and some other guys. Slinked up to me, every part of her tracing curves in the air. She nodded at the can I was holding. "Can I have a sip?"

I almost told her there was plenty of beer on the table, but then I realized that wasn't what she was after. I held out the can. "Sure."

She took a sip, handed it to me, then pulled it back. "Oops. Sorry. Got lipstick on it." She started rubbing off the red mark with her fingertip, then smiled. "Unless you want me to leave it there."

So we started going out. We got into it pretty good, making out, touching, driving each other crazy. One night I started unzipping her jeans. She put her hand on mine. "Brendan," she said breathily, "I don't do that."

I looked at her. "Oh, really? That's not what Tyler Martin said." He was soccer.

She turned red. "That jerk!" Then she shrugged. "Well, okay then. But use a condom. And promise not to tell anybody."

So we did it all the time after that, in my basement, in her basement, in the backseat of my parents' car. And I have to tell you I felt pretty good about it. Here I was, cruising through my senior year, captain of the basketball team, getting laid by the prettiest girl in school, on track for a basketball scholarship and maybe, someday, dream of dreams, the NBA.

This one night we're fooling around on the couch in her rec room. We're kissing and touching and Cassie starts moaning in the back of her throat in that sexy way she has, and nothing is happening. I mean, I'm as limp as the proverbial wet noodle. I haven't been feeling well lately, I've been tired, dragging my ass into school, and I can hardly get myself off the floor to make my jump shots. I've noticed that I look like hell, pale and thin, so I've stopped looking in mirrors.

But *this* is really weird. It's never happened before. I shift position to let

Cassie rub herself against me. She starts unbuttoning her shirt, breathing those short warm breaths on my neck that tell me she's ready. But still nothing is happening. And this is totally bizarre because normally I just have to smell her hair to get a boner.

Finally I know it's not going to happen. Gently, I push Cassie away. "Uh...you know what? I don't feel so hot. We'd better not."

A look of disappointment flickers over her face. Then she puts on a smile. "That's okay, Bren." She looks concerned. "I hope you're not coming down with something."

That was when I knew something was wrong. The next time my mom pestered me about seeing the doctor, I agreed to go.

Now, in the doctor's office, my mom bursts into tears. Dr. Wong starts filling out hospital admission forms. My heart pounds. The word bounces around in my brain like a song you can't get out of your head.

Leukemia. Leukemia. Leukemia.

Chapter Two

The family descends. Literally. My sister Maureen, heavy with child, as they say in my grandparents' Bible, flies in from Calgary. Grandma and Grandpa, my mom's parents, drive in from their retirement village in Kelowna. They're dressed, as usual, in matching golf outfits—white pants, peach-colored shirts and spotless white shoes. Nana, my dad's mom, takes the ferry over from Victoria.

We all sit in the living room. We're pretty squished, and I offer to sit on the floor, but they won't hear of it.

"Not in your condition, honey," Grandma says.

It's been like this. Kid gloves. My parents have been hovering, doing everything for me. Pouring my cereal. Making my bed. It would be funny if it wasn't so tragic.

"Would anybody like something to drink?" my mom asks.

Everybody says they're fine.

"You should have something, Bren," Maureen says.

"I don't want anything."

"Milk? Juice? Something to keep your strength up."

"I'm not thirsty!" I snap.

Everybody looks at me. *Temper, temper.*

Not like you, Brendan, I see them thinking.

Screw it, I think. This little gathering wasn't my idea. Let's just get it over with.

My mom jumps up and starts passing around stacks of paper. "I downloaded information about leukemia, so you'll know what it's about."

My mom is one of those people who believe that the key to tackling any problem is to study it. Collect the facts and analyze the crap out of them. After falling apart in the doctor's office, she pulled herself together and sprang into action. Surfing the Net, downloading, photocopying everything there is to know about acute lymphocytic leukemia, or ALL. Within two days, her conversation was all about lymphocytes and neutrophils and induction therapy.

Meanwhile, my dad's been a wreck. I hear him sobbing behind closed doors.

He comes out red-eyed, forcing a smile, patting me on the back and saying, "Everything'll be fine, Bren." Like he's trying to convince himself, not me. Freaks me out.

Nana leafs through the stapled pages. "Says here that Brendan's type of leukemia has a very high remission rate." She scans the room. "That's good, isn't it?"

I can't look at her. Nana is a tall, broad-shouldered woman—should have been a linebacker, my dad and I often joke. She has a deep, husky smoker's voice, drinks vodka and swears like a sailor. She's famous in our family for getting stinking drunk at Maureen's wedding and trying to do a striptease in the middle of the dance floor. (Fortunately she only got as far as flinging her shoes and earrings into the crowd before my dad hustled her out of there.)

But now her eyes are rimmed with red and her face sags. Every so often she turns away and those massive shoulders shake. I can't stand seeing her cry. Nana never cries. It threatens to bring back my own tears—I've pretty much been a faucet the last few days. When I'm not swearing and throwing stuff across the room, that is.

"Ninety-five percent," my mom announces, pointing at the statistic.

"Yes, that's very positive," my dad says, his voice quivering.

Grandpa nods. "The odds of beating it are excellent."

Grandma pats my leg. "You'll be fine, Brendan."

Oh yeah? I think. And just how do you know that?

"You'll fight this. And win," Maureen says, fixing me with that big-sister glare. Like, you better do what I say or else.

"And we'll be fighting with you, Brendan, every step of the way," Grandpa says.

Bull, I think. Are they going to go through chemo with me? Puke? Lose their hair? Maybe go sterile? Maybe die? No way. That's a road I'm going down alone.

"Lily Taranoff?" Grandma says. "Who lives two units down from us? Her granddaughter had leukemia. Just a little tyke she was. But she beat it, and now she's fine."

Everyone nods.

"My boss's nephew," Maureen says. "Same story. Cancer-free going on seven years."

"See, Bren?" my dad says. "It'll be the same with you."

I start fidgeting. I can't take much more of this.

They start talking about my chemo-therapy schedule and how they're all going to visit me in the hospital. I tune it out. I don't want to think about it.

Don't want to think about getting poison shot into my veins instead of leading my team to the regionals. Or hanging out with Kesh, my best friend. Or getting laid. Or riding my bike or going out for breakfast or any one of the millions of things I won't be able to do for months. If I'm lucky.

The voices die down. Figuring we're done, I stand up.

Grandma pulls me down. "Wait, honey. Before you go, let us pray."

She bows her head. Grandpa follows suit. They sit there with their hands folded.

Everybody else bows their head and folds their hands. Even Nana. That kills me. Normally Nana would be snorting and making sarcastic remarks under her breath.

"Dear merciful God in heaven," Grandma begins.

Merciful?

She goes into a long ramble in which she beseeches the Lord to watch over and protect and bring comfort to "your young servant." She prays that I'll be as receptive to the wondrous healing of our Lord as I surely will be to the medical blessings I'm about to receive. "And let us say—"

I can't take it anymore. I stagger to my feet. "Blessings?" I shout. "Wondrous healing? Bull. If there is a God—and right now it's not looking like it—he's dealt me a rotten hand. Screw prayers!"

I storm out of the room, ignoring the shocked faces that stare at me as I pass.

Chapter Three

There's a knock on my bedroom door. I quickly shove the sheaf of papers under my pillow. I've swiped one of Mom's information packages and have been reading up on the crazy, out-of-control cancer cells in my blood and bone marrow, and how they're wiping out my healthy cells. "Yeah?" I call.

Only my voice is so hoarse that it's a croak. I try again. "Yeah?"

Kesh sticks his head around the door.

I love this guy, all six-foot-four skinny brown beanpole of him. We've been best friends since we were little. We dig the same movies, full of farting and car crashes. Think an entire day spent practicing spinning jump shots is a holiday. Consider pizza and a milk-shake the perfect breakfast. Don't have to say anything to know what the other guy is thinking.

But I don't want to see him. What are we supposed to say to each other? Talk about school, regular stuff, as if everything is normal? And if he starts handing me that crap about how I'm going to be fine, I'm gonna slug him.

Kesh sits on the edge of my bed. Doesn't look at me. Doesn't say anything. Finally he says, "Sucks."

"You got that right."

"Man, I'm so sorry." His voice cracks a little.

"Not as sorry as I am," I snap.

Kesh looks wounded. "Why're you taking it out on me?"

"I'm sick of hearing how sorry everybody is. Being sorry doesn't help. It just weighs me down."

"Well, what am I supposed to say?" he asks.

"I don't know. Just don't give me any pity."

There's silence. Kesh darts me a look, as if he's not sure if he should speak. "Everybody's really upset. Coach was in tears when he told the guys."

My throat feels thick. I swallow.

"Practice isn't the same without you," he says.

"Yeah, well, better get used to it. I don't know when I'll be back." Or *if* I'll be back. Something occurs to me. "Coach name somebody else captain?"

Kesh looks uneasy. "Yeah."

"Who?" I ask.

A pause. "Me."

"Congratulations," I say bitterly.

"I didn't want it!"

"Yeah, right."

"Not like this! Christ. What do you think I am?"

I know I'm being a prick. I know Kesh isn't like that. It's just so goddamn unfair.

"So...what's gonna happen?" he asks.

I tell him about my treatment. How I'm going into the hospital next week. First I'll have a bone-marrow biopsy. That's to confirm that I have ALL. Then I'll have a catheter inserted in my chest to pump the chemo solution into. Then I'll get a wallop of chemo for a solid week.

"It's gonna be brutal," I say. I don't tell him I've memorized the side effects of chemo. Nausea. Hair loss. Mouth sores. Or that I'm scared to death. What if I can't handle it?

"And then?"

"And then we wait and see if it comes back." That's the kicker. That's what's keeping me up at night. Not that I have cancer. Not that I have to go into the hospital. Not that I'm gonna feel like crap. It's this: What if I go through all that...*and it doesn't work?*

My eyes sting. Here come the tears again. I jerk my head aside.

Not quick enough.

"Hey, man, it's okay." Kesh puts his hand on my shoulder. "You can—"

I twist, shaking his hand off. "Get away. Leave me alone."

"Bren, you don't have to be embarr—"

"Didn't you hear me? Get lost!"

There's a stunned silence. Without a word, he gets up and leaves the room.

I shove my face into the pillow, sobbing. Stuff a corner in my mouth so no one will hear.

Chapter Four

"Hey, man."

"Brendan...sorry to hear the news..."

I'm back at school. Not to attend classes, just to talk to my teachers and arrange to get the homework. Though I probably won't feel up to doing it and probably won't be able to graduate with my class. Yet another thing that sucks.

"Hey, buddy, we're pulling for you…"

I'm certainly the sensation of the school. Some kids come over and awkwardly pat me on the back. Some turn away, whispering to their friends. Some hug me. I wish they'd all quit.

I'm just freeing myself from the embrace of my buddy Seth when there's a screech and the sound of clattering heels. "Brendan!" The next minute Cassie throws her arms around me and starts bawling.

"Oh, Bren, you poor thing, it's so terrible—"

She cries, pushing her face against my chest.

"I've been so worried, I haven't been sleeping…or eating…"

Gripping me, she sobs loudly. I stand there, arms at my sides. Finally she lets go. She wipes her eyes, careful to dab under her eyes so her makeup won't run.

"Oh, Bren, when I heard the news I just—I was hysterical. But I want you to know, I'm there for you. I mean it, Bren. No matter what." She gives a quick glance around, then lifts tear-filled eyes to me.

It hits me. Cassie is actually enjoying this. I mean, I know she cares. I know she's worried about me. But I can see that she's also really into her role—Frantically Worried But Loyal Girlfriend. This part has it all. Drama. Tears. Hysteria.

I pat her arm. "Good one, Cassie."

"What do you mean?"

"The grieving girlfriend. Good show."

Her face turns red. "How can you say that? I'm really upset!"

I nod. "I know you are. Especially when you have an audience."

"That is so—so—" She dashes a hand at her eyes again, quickly checking for smudges. "You bastard!"

She storms down the hall.

At the end of the day, I duck into the locker room before practice to say goodbye to Coach. I don't feel like seeing my teammates, getting more sympathy, being reminded of what I'm missing, but I figure I owe it to Coach.

When I arrive, the usual razzing is going on. Guys are chucking smelly jocks at one another, shoving each other off the bench, calling each other names.

"You gonna make any free throws today, Petrowski?"

"You gonna *touch* the ball, douchebag?"

I love this place. The banter, the sweat, even the stink. Guys working together.

The *thwack* of the ball against hardwood. The ball flying from hand to hand as if on invisible strings.

I stick my head in. Conversation stops. Some guys stare at me. A few throats clear. Across the room, Kesh catches my eye, then looks away.

We stay in this horrible frozen silence. Coach bursts in. "Why's it so quiet? Somebody die?"

The words hang in the air. He turns red. "Oh—Brendan—" He blinks fast.

Oh god, don't let me cry.

In two strides he's across the room and hugging me. He lets go, clears his throat. Pats me on the back. "We're gonna win for you, son."

"Yeah...you bet," some of the guys echo.

"And we're gonna carry you into every game and help you get better," Coach adds. "Show him, boys."

The players reach into their lockers

and hold up their game jerseys. Sewn onto the left shoulder of each one, right above the heart, is a blue ribbon in the shape of a *C*. For Captain.

I know this is really nice. It's a sweet idea. Someone went to a lot of trouble to sew on the little ribbons.

But all I can think is, Screw this. I don't want these stupid ribbons standing in for me. I want to be on the court myself, battling for the title. I'm freaking jealous of every one of these guys. Even the ones who're gonna sit on the bench.

I can't speak. If I say anything, it's gonna sound ungrateful, and I don't mean that. I just want to punch something.

I turn away.

"What the—?" someone says.

"Bastard," Petrowski says under his breath.

"Shut up!" Kesh says.

I keep walking, tears stinging my eyes.

Chapter Five

PEDIATRIC ONCOLOGY it says in gold letters on the glass doors to the ward.

I want to puke.

The waiting area is brightly painted with clowns and balloons and smiling dolphins. There's a stack of puzzles and baskets of Lego and puppets in the corner, and a shelf of picture books. It's kiddie-land. I feel like a freak.

A little boy, maybe seven, skinny and bald, in pajamas and slippers, walks slowly across the room, clutching a nurse with one hand and an IV stand with the other. A girl, four or five, naps curled on her mom's lap, thumb in mouth. Two others, one bald, one with a fuzz of brown hair, are on the floor, giggling over a comic book.

My parents and I are met by a nurse who introduces herself as Harjit Sangha. She takes my information and fills out forms. Then she stands up. "Would you like a tour of the ward before I take you to your room?"

No, I think, but my mom says, "Yes, please," before I can answer.

So Nurse Sangha shows us the patient lounge, where there are some couches and a small fridge and a TV, and the radiation rooms and the chemotherapy rooms.

"Your new home-away-from-home," she says to me with a wry smile. "The décor stinks, but at least the chairs are comfortable."

In spite of myself, I smile back. I like her.

As we walk back down the hall toward my room, I see a kid come out of the elevator with a couple of adults. It's a girl, I think, though she's wearing a tuque. She looks about my age, though I can't tell for sure. She's tiny—but then, everyone around here looks shrunken. They walk toward the admitting desk, and we turn down the hall.

My room is typical hospital blah. Cupboard, bed, TV, nightstand. Puke green walls, mud brown bedspread. At least I have a window. I can watch the rain fall.

While I unpack my stuff—clothes, schoolbooks, team picture—Nurse Sangha explains what's going to happen when my chemotherapy starts.

At least she's trying to. My mom keeps cutting in. "With ALL, intrathecal chemotherapy is recommended, correct?"

Nurse Sangha smiles. "You've been doing your homework, Mrs. Halleran."

My mom brandishes her papers. "Yes. I understand that central nervous system prophylaxis is very important—"

Nurse Sangha nods. Her smile dims a little. "Yes, and we are aware of that. If the biopsy confirms ALL, Brendan will start with systemic induction therapy for the first round of treatments. CNS prophylaxis comes in the second phase."

My dad goes into the bathroom. I hear the water running, hard, and the toilet flushing at the same time.

There's a long pause. He comes out, red-eyed, not looking at me.

I want to scream at him to cut it out. Yeah, I know he's worried. But *I'm* the one who needs to fall apart. I want to curl up in his lap and howl. But I can't, because I'm afraid to make him worse. Because every time I see him, he gives me the fake smile and the pat on the back, and even though I want to tell him to stop the bull, I can't. And I can't get through to my mom either. All she does is burrow into the Internet, wave paper around, spout facts and figures.

Even now. "And I believe the dosage will be—"

Nurse Sangha puts up her hand. "We've got it all figured out, Mrs. Halleran. And now"—before my mom can jump in again—"I think Brendan needs some rest."

After many hugs and a few tears and promises to be here first thing tomorrow, they leave. Nurse Sangha shoots me a conspiratorial smile, as if to say, *Finally.*

I can't help but smile back.

"Anything I can do for you?"

I shake my head. She leaves. I lie back and enjoy the peace and quiet.

For exactly one minute. Then the questions come flooding back.

What will the chemo feel like? Will it hurt? Will I puke uncontrollably? What if I can't stop? What if I can't stand the pain? What if I make an ass of myself?

What if it doesn't work?

Tears prick. God, I'm such a crybaby and I can't help it and this is so unfair and I don't want to wake up tomorrow—no, wait! Yes, I do! I didn't mean that! And then I'm bawling into my pillow, and I almost don't hear it, but I do. The faint sound of a doorknob turning.

I look over my shoulder. The door opens. A bald head peeks around.

"Mind if I come in?" it says. I don't know if it's a he or she.

"Well, actually—," I begin. Because I do mind. I'm a seventeen-year-old guy bawling his eyes out, and I don't feel like seeing anybody.

"Harj told me there was someone else my age on the ward."

"Harj?" I ask in spite of myself.

"Harjit. Nurse Sangha."

"You're on a first-name basis?"

He—she—beams me a smile. "You spend as much time in here as I do, and you will be too."

The person comes all the way into the room. It takes me a minute to realize it's the girl I saw come in earlier. She had a hat on then. Now her head is bald. No, it's not, I see as she comes closer. There's a fine layer of blond fuzz all over it. Her eyes, blue-gray, are huge in her thin face. She's wearing a long-sleeved maroon T and navy yoga pants.

Her collarbone and hip bones jut out. She's flat-chested. I can't tell if she's twelve or twenty-five.

She comes over to the bed. Holds out her hand. "I'm Lark."

"Brendan," I say, shaking her hand.

"Yeah, I know—"

"Don't tell me. Harj told you."

She laughs. It's like a bell, high and tinkling.

She starts walking around the room, looking at my stuff. The picture of my basketball team, the clipping about the regionals. My iPod. A plate of peanut-butter cookies, my all-time favorite, which my mom baked, trying to tempt me to eat, and which I haven't touched. The detective novel I'm reading when my headache isn't too bad. She picks that up and looks at the spine.

At first I stiffen. Who the hell does she think she is, touching my stuff? But then I realize that I don't actually mind.

It's kind of soothing, watching her glide around the room like a butterfly, landing first on this flower, then on the next.

"So," she says, "ALL?" She sits on the edge of the bed. It hardly sags.

"Don't know. Bone-marrow biopsy tomorrow." *Does it hurt?* I want to know but am too embarrassed to ask. "You?"

She nods. "I've had two chemo cycles. Didn't work."

"Holy shit." It slips out before I can stop myself.

But she smiles. "Holy shit is right. I'm in for a bone-marrow transplant. Last chance. Do or die." She pauses. "Probably die."

I can't believe this. They only do bone-marrow transplants if the outlook is really bad. Yet she's talking about it so calmly, as if we were having a casual conversation. Seen any good movies lately? No, you?

For a moment I wonder if she's not

quite all there. Maybe the chemo did something to her brain.

She glides over to the window, pushes aside the curtain. It's dark out. I can see her pale reflection in the glass. There are drops of water on the outside.

She sighs. "I love the rain. Especially when it's windy and the rain is driving into your face, and you're all shivery, and you have to lean into the wind or it'll knock you over, and you get soaked and chilled and have goose bumps all over, and then you come inside and put on dry clothes and thick socks and have cocoa, and the rain is drumming on the roof and it's cozy and warm." She turns. "Don't you?"

"What the hell!" I explode.

She gapes at me. "What?"

"Are you for real? Are you crazy?"

She comes back toward the bed. "I don't think so." She smiles. "Well, maybe a little."

That pushes me further over the edge. "You have cancer. I have cancer. We might die. How can you talk about the rain?"

She sits down and takes my hand. "Why not? Was there something else you wanted to talk about?"

"No!" I fling her hand away. "How can you be so calm? It's unreal."

She pauses. "What else can I do? Besides, I do love the rain. And the sun and the wind and the snow."

I jump up, pace across the room, then turn and glare at her. "Well, I don't believe it. And I don't feel like talking about it. All this…love…and cocoa… it's bull!" My head is pounding.

Lark gets up. "I didn't mean to upset you, Brendan."

"Well, you did!"

A stricken look crosses her face. "I'm sorry."

"Just go."

A pause. "All right. Good night, Brendan." She floats across the room and is gone.

I pace. Of all the crazy, frustrating—

How on earth does anybody expect me to believe—?

She's dying and she's smiling and going on about how wonderful the rain is? No way. Either she's full of it, just trying to distract herself, keep the fear down, or she's nuts, soft in the head, or she's putting on an act, trying to impress me—

I stop. She didn't seem crazy. Or fake. She seemed real.

But it's impossible, I tell myself. It must be bullshit.

I fling myself into bed, seeing that strange pale smile in the glass.

It's a long time before I fall asleep.

Chapter Six

I have the bone-marrow biopsy. A needle inserted in my hip bone. It hurts like hell at first. Then it's just a dull ache.

It takes a couple of days to get the results. Meanwhile, I find out I'm anemic. That's why I've been dragging my ass for weeks. So I have to get blood transfusions. That's a load of fun.

The biopsy confirms that I have ALL. The most common—and fastest-growing—type. So I'm going to start chemo. Two drugs at once, one 24/7 for a week and the other on three days for an hour. A huge blast of chemicals to knock out all the bad cells. Only problem is, they knock out the good cells, plus my bone marrow, at the same time.

I'm scared.

I start chemo. It doesn't hurt—that's a relief—but it's brutal lying back in a reclining chair watching liquid poison slowly drip through a bag into your catheter, into your veins. Hours of boredom. And fear.

And the whole time I have my parents yammering at me. I tried to tell them they didn't have to stay, but they wouldn't hear of leaving me to face it alone. So here they are, each holding one of my hands, talking across me in dueling conversations.

"Daunorubicin is very effective at finding and destroying lymphoblasts—," my mom begins.

"Marcia, I don't think Brendan wants to hear about the drugs right now," my dad interrupts.

"But he needs to be involved in his treatment. It's a critical factor in fighting the disease. Studies show—"

"I don't think—"

"Shut up!" I shout. They both look at me. We don't say that in our house. Don't raise our voices. But I can't stand this. "Just stop talking. I don't want to hear anything."

There's a stunned silence. The only sound is the murmur of voices in the hall, the almost imperceptible *beep-beep-beep* of the machine as it monitors the flow of chemicals. We sit like that, my parents holding my hands, their lips compressed, while one bag empties and another is put in its place.

After I'm finished getting the "three" drug—the one I'm getting three doses of—Nurse Sangha says I can continue with the "seven" drug in my room. So, pushing my IV stand, I pad down the hall and get into bed. I try to get my parents to leave, but they insist on staying, even though Nurse Sangha tells them I'll probably just sleep most of the day.

They sit in the chairs beside the bed. "Well, Bren, that's the first step toward remission," my dad says in his fake-hearty voice.

"Yes." My mom brightens. "In eighty-five percent of cases, there's a steep decline in blast cells after only one week of treatments."

"So you just have to stay positive—"

I want to scream. But I don't, because suddenly I have to puke. I push my call button.

"What's the matter, Bren?" my dad says.

I just shake my head. I don't want to open my mouth.

Nurse Sangha rushes in, takes one look at me, reaches into a cupboard and hands me a plastic bucket. I grab it and heave. Even though I haven't eaten all day, slimy yellow gunk comes up. I spew, breathe hard, sweat, spew again.

"Oh, Brendan. Here, let me." My mom tries to wipe my forehead. I whip my head to push her hand away.

When I'm finished, Nurse Sangha takes the bucket away. She returns with a wet washcloth and wipes my face. Gingerly I go into the bathroom and brush my teeth, then get back into bed.

Nurse Sangha hands me a couple of

pills and a glass of water. "Well, now we know," she says dryly, giving me a sympathetic look. She hands me a clean bucket. "Meet your new best friend."

I manage to smile back. They hadn't given me anti-nausea medication before the chemo in case I didn't need it—not everyone gets sick, and you're better off taking fewer meds rather than more. But I guess I'm one of the unlucky ones.

I take the pills, then curl up on my side, my back to my parents. My dad reaches over and starts smoothing my hair back from my forehead. My mom comes around in front of me with the bucket. "Do you need this, Bren? Want me to put it here? Or on the night table?"

I want her to shut up. I want my dad to tuck me in and kiss me good night, like he used to do when I was little. My mom always slept like a log, so my dad was the one Maureen and I went to when we had a bad dream or had a fever or had to throw up. He sponged us down, cleaned us up, changed our pajamas, carried us to bed. My arms tight around his neck, my legs wrapped around his waist. His warm hands stroking my back. His whisper, "You'll be fine now." And I always was.

That's what I want. And I feel like such a wuss. And I hate feeling like that.

I shove the bucket away, wiggle away from my dad's hand.

"Just leave me alone."

"But honey—"

"Go."

Silence.

A whisper I can't hear. The rustle of their coats.

"We'll see you tomorrow, Brendan."

"If there's anything you need…" My dad's voice trails off.

I don't answer. They leave. I curl up tighter on the bed, hugging the bucket.

Chapter Seven

An hour later I'm half lying, half sitting up in bed, holding the bucket. The nausea meds haven't kicked in yet. If I lie all the way down, the nausea gets worse. If I sit up, my head hurts.

My stomach heaves. I lean on an elbow and retch. Again. Wipe my mouth. Rinse with water, spit. The water swirls over the brownish puke. Yesterday's lentil soup, the odd orange fleck of carrot.

Nurse Sangha cleans out the bucket, brings me my toothbrush. I spit in a basin. Close my eyes. My head swims. I open them. Stare at the blank TV screen. There's nothing on but kids' cartoons and talk shows. I know. I've checked.

This sucks. I can't read, can't talk, can't do anything. Nausea has taken over my world like an unwelcome guest who won't leave.

There's a tap on the door. It opens. Lark.

"Can I come in?"

I don't feel like company, least of all her and her fake happiness. But maybe she'll distract me. I beckon with my pinkie finger.

She stands by the bed. "Bucket blues, huh?"

I start to nod, then stop. Even that motion makes it worse.

"Poor boy. I remember it well."

I look at her. Think about how she's gone through this twice. Two multiplied by seven days by twenty-four hours. I don't even want to think about how many hours of nausea that was, how many buckets she must have filled. How did she get through it?

She touches my forehead. Her fingers are cool. "I can help," she says. "Wait here."

I snort. As if I'm going anywhere.

She disappears, then comes back a minute later with a turquoise bedspread— where did that come from? I wonder. It sure isn't the standard hospital brown— which she flaps open and spreads on the floor. She puts the bucket on one side of the bedspread, then says, "Up."

I don't want to move. "Can't."

"Yes, you can. Slowly."

I honestly don't think I can move, but she takes me by the shoulders, and damned if she doesn't have me sitting up in a moment. Taking me by one hand, pushing my IV stand with the other, she leads me over to the bedspread.

"What the—?"

"Trust me."

Trust this hippy-dippy flower child who's so full of it she believes her own delusions? Not likely. But I don't have much choice. I shuffle over to the edge of the bedspread. She lies facedown on one side and motions for me to lie on the other.

"Are you crazy?"

"Come on. It'll help. Really."

Feeling like a fool, I lie on my stomach beside her, my IV line snaking beside me. "Now what?"

She doesn't answer. She reaches into her pocket and pulls out an iPod. Slips one earbud into her ear and the other into mine.

What's coming? I wonder. Some kind of brainwashing? Some new-age "you are beautiful and all is well" crap?

Soft music starts playing. A tinkling piano, a quiet sultry sax, a brush sliding over a drum. A woman's voice starts singing:

"Ooh, ooh, ooh, what a little moonlight can do,

Ooh, ooh, ooh, what a little moonlight can do to you..."

I've heard the voice before. Husky. A little gravelly. Like soft, worn velvet. I look at Lark.

"Billie Holiday."

That's it. My dad listens to her sometimes.

"Wait a while, till a little moonbeam comes peepin' through..."

The song is great. I like the easy, swinging beat. But I feel like an idiot, lying on the floor, sharing an iPod with a girl I don't even know. Is this supposed to cure my nausea? That's nuts. And there must be all kinds of germs on the floor, and chemo patients are supposed to avoid germs.

I reach up to pull out the earbud, but Lark puts her hand on mine. "Wait. Give it a chance."

"This is stupid—"

"Don't you like the music?"

I do like the music. The band is cruising along, and Billie is pouring her heart out in every bent note. That doesn't make me feel less like a jerk. Still, I feel the groove. Okay, one more song, I tell myself. Then I'm out of here.

The song changes. This one's slower, moodier.

"Mama may have...Papa may have...

But God bless the child who's got his own...who's got his own..."

I close my eyes. Hear the pain in Billie's voice, but something more, underneath. Joy. Strength. As if to say, Life's a bitch, so what else can you do but sing?

My breathing slows. I feel my weight sink into the floor, my cheek pressing against the bedspread. It's soft and cottony and smells faintly of peppermint. I open my eyes. Lark's staring at me. Her eyes are blue-gray beams. There are tiny flecks of brown in them. A faint smile is on her lips.

This is too weird. What the hell is going on? I think. Who is Lark? What's her story? I feel like there's some kind of con going on, some trick she's pulling. I don't trust this.

But I can't resist. Billie croons, *"Willow, weep for me..."* Her voice takes me by the hand and leads me someplace quiet. My heartbeat slows, keeping time with the drum. And I realize that I haven't thought about throwing up for several minutes. It's not like I'm cured—my stomach is still unsettled—but I'm distracted. Relaxed.

"Bend your branches down upon the ground and cover me..."

Lark's hand edges over toward mine. Our fingers touch.

I close my eyes.

Chapter Eight

Minutes, hours, days of chemo. I'm tied to my IV line like a prisoner to his chains. One after another, the bags empty. I sleep, try to read, look out the window, sleep. Try not to think about basketball, Kesh, my team.

Amazingly, the anti-nausea meds work. I still feel queasy, and I have no appetite, but I'm not barfing like I did at the beginning.

Finally my chemo is done. When they take the IV line out, I feel like a dog who's been let off the leash for the first time in days. I'm so happy I could dance—except I have no energy. Zilch. I feel like I've been flattened by a linebacker. I lie there, trying to muster the energy to get up and go to the bathroom. It's only because I'm so sick of the bedpan that I force myself to do it.

Now I have to wait several weeks for my healthy bone marrow to grow—and to see if the leukemia comes back.

I have blood tests almost every day. Of course my blood counts are really low because the chemo wiped out all my healthy cells. I have no defenses. An infection could kill me. Every time the blood test results come back, I hold my breath.

So far so good.

I don't see Lark for a couple of days. And when I think back to that day, I almost wonder if I imagined the whole thing. Lying on the floor, getting blissed out to jazz? Too weird. I wonder, half-seriously, if Lark hypnotized me. Then I tell myself not to be stupid. She showed me a way to fight nausea. End of story.

I'm coming back to my room when I notice her door's open. I haven't been inside, but I know it's her room.

I peek in. See a purple cloud over the bed. What the—?

"Brendan!"

I turn to go. "I was just—"

"Come on in."

I hesitate, then push open the door. Wow. The purple is a kind of canopy she has made by draping gauzy scarves from poles, transforming the bed into a violet cocoon, and she's sitting in the middle of it, on the turquoise bedspread. On the night table is a blown-glass vase full of sunflowers. A peacock feather dangles from the TV knob. On the walls are pictures: a ballerina in a tutu; a pair of penguins with their chick, a ball of gray down, cradled between their feet; children's faces smeared with chocolate ice cream; a mountain stream tumbling over boulders. Some funky woven thing, in shades of red and gold, is draped over the clothes cupboard. It's like she has created her own private art gallery in here. In her hospital room.

Unaccountably, I'm angry. I make a disgusted noise.

"What?" she asks.

"What's the point?" I shout.

"W-what?"

I sweep my arm to the side. "This. All this—stuff. Why bother?"

Lark looks at me like I'm crazy. "Because it's beautiful."

"But it's a hospital room!"

"Yeah, that's the point." She sits up, crossing her legs. "If I have to spend time in here, why not fill it with beauty?"

"Because—because it's a waste of time."

She gives me a pitying look. "Of course it's not. Every night I drift off to purple dreams. Everywhere I look, I see things I love. What could be better?"

I shake my head. "I can't talk to you."

"Why not?"

"Because you make me feel like crap."

"I do? Why?" She sounds distressed.

"Because you're—a saint! Everything is so perfect with you. It's inhuman!" I turn to go.

Behind me, I hear a peal of laughter. I turn. She's sitting on the bed, holding herself, laughing.

Now she's making fun of me? Screw this. I turn again.

"No!" she says between giggles. "Wait, Brendan. Please. It's just— a saint!" She bursts out again.

I cross the room toward her. "Well, you are. You're in this crazy, blissed-out state. Aren't you afraid, for Christ's sake?"

"Of course I am," she says quietly.

"Then how—?"

She pats the bed next to her. After a moment I sit down. We're both inside the purple tent. On Lark's lap is a well-worn yellow sheep with a wooly head of curls.

"Of course I want to live," she says, looking me in the face. "More than anything. I want to have babies and travel the world and fall in love and dance and read a million books and get drunk and get old. And I know my chances are slim. And that makes me sad."

"See? That's exactly what I mean!" I say, exasperated. " 'That makes me sad.'

You're so calm." I jab my finger at her. "How old are you anyway?"

"Sixteen. Why?"

I roll my eyes. "Sixteen? You seem like a wise old lady. How can you be like that? I go around practically crapping my pants, I'm so scared."

Lark gives me a sympathetic smile. "Don't you think I've been there too?"

"No!"

She shakes her head. "Believe me, I have. When I got diagnosed, I was a wreck. Cried for days. Weeks. I threw tantrums. I was so mad. Why me? It's not fair. I told God to go screw himself."

I can't help but smile. "You?"

"Me. I was miserable. Made everyone around me miserable."

Sounds familiar, I think.

She goes on. "But you know what? After a while I got tired of it. It was like being all black inside. Who wants to be filled with blackness? So I put it down."

"But how? You can't just—"

She shrugs. "I don't know. Maybe I just blew it out of my system."

"But—"

"Listen, Brendan." She takes my hands in hers. "I don't want to die. I want the transplant to work. But I decided that, however much time I have left, I don't want to spend it being angry and miserable. It's a waste of energy—and I don't have enough energy to waste."

I listen to her words. Let them sink in. Maybe they make sense for her. But they sure as hell don't for me. I shake my head. "I couldn't—"

"Sure you could."

I think about it. Try to imagine walking away from my fear and anger, just leaving them by the side of the road like an unwanted parcel.

No. Impossible.

"Not me."

"You'll see," Lark says.

I push myself to my feet. No. I don't think so. But as I walk to my room, I feel strangely comforted. At least Lark's human. Not some perfect angel.

That makes me feel better.

Chapter Nine

One day I feel a little chill. I shiver. Then I feel hot. I start running a fever.

I've got an infection.

It's like a fire alarm went off. I'm surrounded by nurses taking my temperature, sponging me down, taking blood. I'm put to bed with IV antibiotics. They're hovering over me so much, it freaks me out.

Then it hits me. I could beat the leukemia, wipe out all the bad cells, only to be killed by a freaking infection?

That really pisses me off.

I'm lucky. The antibiotics work. After a day or two, my fever comes down. The infection is beaten.

This time.

When I'm able to walk around again, I go looking for Lark. She's not in her room. I ask Harjit, and she tells me that Lark's started preparation for her bone-marrow transplant. She has to get high-dose chemotherapy and total body irradiation for a week and a half. That's to completely wipe out her immune system so her body won't reject the donor's bone marrow.

I try not to think of her with no immune system.

Next time I check, she's there. She's in black yoga pants and a lime green polo shirt. Her back's to me, and her shoulder blades stick out. There's nothing to her, and for the first time I wonder if she's strong enough to get through the operation.

She's standing in the middle of the room, both arms overhead, the IV line trailing from under her shirt. She reaches up, first with one hand, then the other, her ribs lifting from side to side. I don't want to interrupt, so I turn to go.

"Brendan!"

"Sorry, I didn't know you were—"

"No worries. Come on in."

I go over. There's a little color in her cheeks, and her eyes are bright. "You look good," I say.

"Feel good," she says with a grin. "Haven't thrown up in two whole days."

She stretches again, and she's so light I think she might rise up off the floor.

"Want to meet someone amazing?" she says.

"Uh…sure."

She walks over to the picture of the ballerina and points. "My hero."

I go over and look. The dancer is bent over at the waist, her tutu jutting up behind her. Both arms are curving over her head as if she's pulling up a hood. There's an intense look on her face. Pain? Sadness? I can't tell.

"Who's she?"

"Galina Romanovska."

"Who's that?"

"A Russian ballerina. I saw her dance 'The Dying Swan.' It's a famous piece, very short, only a few minutes long. The swan has been shot, by an arrow. It's dying." Lark looks back at the picture, her eyes far away. "She didn't just portray the swan, she *became* the swan."

One of Lark's arms floats up, and then she makes it tremble, at first quietly, in small fluttery motions, then violently, jerking, and in that instant I know that she's a dancer. In fact, it's so obvious— her lightness, her gracefulness—that I can't believe I didn't realize it sooner.

"She was magnificent," Lark goes on. "The audience clapped so much that she came out and did the whole piece all over again." There are tears in Lark's eyes. "It was the most amazing thing I ever saw."

"Wow."

"Who's *your* hero?"

"I don't know. I guess I don't have one."

"Come on."

I think. Cast my mind through people I know—my dad, teachers, Coach. Then it comes to me. "Steve Nash."

"Steve Nash," Lark repeats. "I've heard that name…"

"You've heard that name!" I say indignantly. "He's only the greatest point guard in the game."

"Sorry. Tell me."

I've seen Steve Nash play maybe a hundred games on TV and even seen him live a few times. I've read about him. I've tried to copy his moves. But I've never tried to put into words what makes him great. It takes a minute. "He's just an incredible playmaker. He can, like, see the game. See the court, see where the action is going to go. Or needs to go. And then he sets it up. As if he has eyes on the sides of his head, like a bird."

"Cool."

"And he's a great shooter too. Just a sweet natural shot. But he's generous. Not a ball hog."

Lark regards me. "That says something about you."

"What do you mean?"

"Admiring that about him."

"Oh, well." I feel myself blushing. I picture Nash in action. "He'll be coming down court," I tell Lark, "dribbling short and hard, keeping control." I mimic the dribbling movements. "His eyes are flicking from left to right, spotting his teammates. He makes a quick feint to the side to brush off the opposing player"—I swivel sharply to the left, then the right—"then makes a perfect pass, right into the hands of the guy under the net, who goes up and—"

My arm goes up. My wrist flicks.

Then I clench my fist and lower it, hard.

"What?" Lark says.

"The regionals," I say tightly. I tell her about how I'm supposed to be there right now, leading my team. "I'm so pissed off. I worked so hard all season. And those guys...they get to play...and win...It's not fair!"

I hear my voice crack. My eyes sting with tears.

"Oh, Brendan," Lark says tenderly.

That does it. All at once I'm bawling, and this stuff comes pouring out, only it's not about being mad. It's completely different. "I'm so scared...I don't want to die..."

Lark puts her arms around my waist. I'm sobbing on her shoulder, holding her, hugging her. "Oh god...oh god..."

She just holds me. I shake with sobs. In all this time I've never cried in front of anyone, not even my parents, and here I am bawling on this tiny girl. I'm choking and sniffling and my tears are mixed with snot and I can't stop.

Finally I do though. I wipe my face with my sleeve. I can't look at her. I want to crawl in a hole.

"Sorry," I say to the floor.

"Oh, Brendan," she says. She takes my hands and I have to look at her.

"It's okay to cry. To be afraid."

"But—"

"It's brave to admit it."

I bark out a laugh. "Brave—that's a joke."

"You cry. You freak out. Then you go on. You take the next breath, and the next. That's brave."

I look at her. I don't know if she's right. I do know one thing though. I don't feel ashamed anymore.

I gather her to me. I hold her delicate, strong body in my arms. I take the next breath.

Chapter Ten

I'm in the bathroom. Absentmindedly, I brush my hands through my hair. And it happens. A hank of hair comes out in my hand.

I expected this. You know it's coming. But still, it's a shock. I've got a bald patch on the side of my head. I look like a freak.

The next day another clump falls out. Then another. My head's a checkerboard. Scalp. Hair. Scalp. Hair. Scalp, scalp, hair. King me. Scalp wins.

And guess what—it's cold without hair. That's another thing about chemo. Your thermostat goes kaput and you alternate between freezing and sweltering. I start wearing a tuque during the cold spells. When I take it off, I find hunks of hair in it.

Harjit must have told my parents that I was down in the dumps, because the next thing I know my whole family— Mom and Dad, Grandma and Grandpa, Nana, Maureen—comes in for a visit. To cheer me up.

Yeah, right.

Nana flinches when she sees my head, which is now completely bald.

She doesn't say anything, but I see her wipe her eyes.

Maureen is even more pregnant, a freighter sailing down the hall. My parents introduce her to Harjit, and everybody jokes that it's a good thing she's in the hospital, just in case. Hilarious.

They crowd into my room. I'm on the bed, my parents and Maureen are on chairs on one side, my grandparents on the other. I feel like a freak on display. Ladies and gentlemen, the bald cancer patient. Observe how he pulls his sweatshirt on and off as his temperature fluctuates.

Right now I'm having a hot spell, so my head is bare.

"The bald look suits you, Bren," Maureen says. "You could go for a shaved head even after you get your hair back."

"Yeah, right."

"You know, you're right, Maureen," Grandpa says. "Brendan has a very nicely shaped head."

"At least you'll get yours back," my dad says, running a hand over his bald spot. "I don't have any hope of that."

Everybody gives a forced laugh.

There's a silence.

"So...how do you feel, honey?" Grandma says.

How do I answer that? Tell the truth or lie? "Like crap."

"Oh, Brendan," my mom says in a distressed tone.

"Well, I do. I'm wiped all the time, I get headaches, and my taste buds are wonky, so food tastes gross." I hear myself complaining and hate the whine in my voice. But they asked.

"That must mean the chemo is working," my mom says brightly.

I roll my eyes and snort.

There's another silence.

I wish they'd leave. I know it's terrible of me, I know they came a long way and took a lot of trouble and all that, but I don't want to be with them. I just want to be with Lark. She doesn't look at me with eyes full of worry. She doesn't lie to me. She's the only one who knows what I'm going through. She speaks my language, thinks my thoughts.

"Well, I think you look good, Bren," Maureen says.

"Doesn't he?" Grandpa says, nodding.

This is such a lie that I almost laugh out loud. I've lost about ten pounds, I have no color and I'm bald. "Bull," I say.

"Brendan!" Grandma scolds. She exchanges a look with Grandpa. Such language. Blasphemy.

"No, I mean it," Maureen says. "You look pretty healthy. I'm sure you're going to pull through this just fine."

"Oh yeah?" I say loudly. "Just how do you know that? Are you the great expert or something?"

Maureen looks like she's been slapped.

"That was uncalled for, Brendan," my mom says, taking Maureen's hand. "Especially after your sister flew all this way to see you."

"And she was just trying to be positive," my dad puts in. "That's what you've got to do, Bren. Keep a positive attitude."

"Okay, sure," I snap. "You try it."

I start feeling cold and jam the tuque back on my head.

My mom jumps up. "Are you cold, honey? Want to get under the covers?"

"No, I'm fine. Isn't that what you just said?"

"Oh, Bren," my mom says, sitting back down, "it's no good being so negative.

78

You've got to keep your spirits up. It's so important."

"Yes!" Nana says excitedly. "I read this book about people getting better from serious illnesses. You know, like being terminal and suddenly being cured?"

"It's the hand of the Lord," Grandma says.

I roll my eyes.

"I don't know about the Lord," Nana says, "but the thing they all had in common was a positive attitude. They *believed* they were going to get better—and they did. I'm telling you, Brendan, that's the ticket."

I feel betrayed. Grandma and Grandpa spouting this crap I can accept. I mean, it drives me crazy, but I expect it from them. But Nana? Wisecracking, sarcastic, foul-mouthed Nana? How can she buy this stuff? And how can she lay it on me?

"That is the stupidest thing I ever heard, and if you guys believe it, you're idiots," I yell.

As soon as the words are out of my mouth, I feel terrible.

"Brendan!" my mom says.

They all stare at me like I'm some kind of monster. Looking hurt, they leave.

Chapter Eleven

Just after the door closes behind my family, I hear a tap.

"Lark!" I grin, happy to see her.

She doesn't grin back.

"What? What's the matter? Are you okay?" I ask, alarmed.

"I heard," she says, fixing those big eyes on me.

"Heard what?"

"You. And your family."

I flush. "They drive me crazy."

She doesn't answer.

"Well, they do," I say irritably. "I can't stand it."

"I didn't say anything."

"You don't have to. I can tell you think I'm an asshole."

She gives a sly smile. "Your words."

"Who are you to judge?" I snap. "Your parents are cool. They don't... hover. You don't have to deal with that crap."

"I'm not judging," she says calmly.

"Well, it sure looks like it."

"Brendan, how you treat people is up to you."

"Yeah, it is! So why don't you just butt out?"

She leaves.

I spend the next day telling myself I don't care what she thinks. That it's none of her goddamn business. That she can take her self-righteous attitude and shove it.

There's only one problem. She's right. I *was* an asshole. I know my family loves me and are scared and don't know what to say. I know they can't help it. I know Nana was only trying to give me hope.

And there's another problem. I miss Lark. I'm miserable without her.

I hold out one whole day and night. The next morning I knock on her door.

"Brendan!" She looks delighted to see me.

Maybe she's forgotten all about it, I think. Maybe I don't have to apologize.

Then—damn. I know I do.

"I just came to say...," I begin, not looking at her, "...that...oh, hell, you were right...and I'm going to try to

be nicer…and I'm sorry for being a jerk."
I take a breath. "There."

There's a silence. I look up.

"You don't have to apologize to me,
Brendan."

"Yeah. I do."

"Okay. Accepted. But it's not about
me. It's about you. About how you want
to live, with whatever time you've got.
That's all."

I don't know what she's talking about.
I don't care. I cross the room. Take her
hands. "Friends?"

She beams. "Friends."

I heave a sigh.

"So, what should we do?" I say.

"I don't know. Watch a movie?"

"Nah. Umm…play cards?"

She shakes her head. We think. Then
Lark brightens. "I know. How's your
stomach?"

"Not too bad."

"Good. Come with me."

Pushing her IV stand, she leads me to the patient lounge. The fridge is stocked with Jell-O and juice and stuff—foods that are easy for chemo patients to tolerate.

Lark takes out several different flavors of pudding. "Let's have a taste test," she says.

"Okay. What do I have to do?"

"Nothing. We just taste different flavors and see what we like."

"Cool." I grab a cup of chocolate, rip off the top and start shoveling it in, but Lark says, "No. Slow down. Really taste it."

So I do. Take a spoonful and hold it in my mouth. Pay attention.

At first all I can taste is the gross, metallic taste I have in my mouth all the time. But then my taste buds start working, and the chocolate starts coming through. It's creamy and dark and rich. A little nutty. A little bitter. A little sweet.

I don't think I've ever tasted chocolate like this, really tasted it. It's like being stoned, only without the drugs.

I grin at Lark. "It's fantastic."

She feeds me a taste of vanilla. I close my eyes and taste the utter creaminess of it. The sweet, smooth milkiness of it.

I try butterscotch. It's caramely. Sweet. Almost burned-tasting. I'm trying to find the words. Then it comes to me. "It tastes like Billie Holiday's voice."

Lark stares at me. Tears come into her eyes. She leans over and kisses me on the cheek.

I don't know what I did to deserve that, but whatever it was, I'm glad I did it.

We go back to Lark's room. She takes out her iPod. "Want to hear my favorite blues song in the whole world?"

I nod. We sit side by side on her bed. She gives me an earbud and puts the other in her own ear. A guitar plays a funky intro. A deep, gravelly voice starts singing, *"I got a little red rooster too lazy to crow for day..."*

The beat is slow. The voice is like scratchy sandpaper. A guitar string twangs on a bent note.

"Keeps all the hens in the barnyard upset in every way..."

I've never really listened to the blues, but all of a sudden I get it. I get the darkness, the minor key. I feel the beat in my blood.

I look at Lark. She smiles. I smile back.

Lark stands up, tucking the iPod in her waistband. She holds out her hands.

I stand. Hands clasped, we sway from side to side, nodding our heads in time.

"If you see my little red rooster, please drive him home..."

I slip my arms around her. She nestles against me. I feel the hump of her catheter, her bony chest. I close my eyes. Her hair smells like peppermint. We sway, barely moving.

I give myself over to the music. To the voice. I don't think I've ever listened so hard. Heard so clearly. Felt another person's body so closely. This isn't about sex, about scoring with a girl.

It's about listening. Dancing. Holding. Right here. Right now.

It's all I need.

Chapter Twelve

Red blood cells live for 120 days. The living ones don't get killed by the chemo, but no new ones grow either. So I'm anemic again. I need more blood transfusions.

See what fascinating scientific information you learn when you have leukemia?

I'm lying around one day, feeling zapped, waiting for the transfusion to give me some energy back, when I hear a commotion in the hall. Loud voices. Heavy footsteps. Laughter.

Harjit knocks on the door. "You up for visitors?"

I nod. Next minute, my basketball team piles into my room. The whole squad, plus Coach. They squeeze around the bed, jostling, telling each other to shove over.

"Watch it," Seth says as Petrowski elbows him aside, "you're pushing me out the window."

"That's the idea," Petrowski says, and everybody laughs.

Then they fall silent when they see my bald head. Their eyes flick everywhere but me.

My dad must have told Coach I was bald, because they bring me a baseball cap emblazoned with the school mascot, the eagle, and my name spelled out in felt letters.

I thank them and put on the cap. Everybody says it looks great. Silence falls again.

They tell me how they've beaten every team in the regionals and are off to the finals next weekend.

"That's great," I say. "Good luck."

Nobody says anything for a minute. I see Coach nudge Petrowski. Looking embarrassed, Petrowski steps forward. He takes something from behind his back. It's a wooden plaque.

"We...uh...since we won the regionals...we...uh...I mean, they gave us this..."

"Way to go, Petrowski, you smooth talker," Seth teases.

There's laughter. Petrowski blushes. He thrusts the plaque into my hands. "It's for you."

MOUNTAINVIEW SECONDARY SCHOOL—REGIONAL CHAMPIONS, it says in fancy letters.

I look up. All their eyes are on me. "Uh...thanks, guys." They continue to stare at me, as if waiting for me to say more. I can't think of anything else to say. It's not like I don't appreciate it. I do. It's a really nice gesture. It's just that I've just realized that I've hardly thought about basketball, the finals, the competition lately. They all seem far away from me now. I've got bigger things to worry about. Every day is an obstacle to get through. Every day is a victory.

Finally everybody leaves but Kesh. He starts telling me about the game last week against Eastside, our biggest rival. Normally I'd be hanging on every word. I'm only half paying attention.

"...and Coach said it was our best defensive game of the year..."

It takes me a minute to realize he's stopped. "What?"

"You're not listening."

I don't respond to that. Instead I say, "I met a girl."

He looks surprised. "Here? In the hospital?"

"Yeah."

He wags his finger. "Cassie's gonna be pissed."

I snort and roll my eyes. As if Cassie matters.

"Whoa, you mean it." Kesh gives me a sleazy grin. "So, is she hot?"

I glare at him. "It's not like that."

"No?"

"No!"

"Hey, sorry. So it's like, what, just friends?" He looks doubtful, as if he doesn't believe I could meet a girl without wanting to get in her pants.

"Yeah!"

"Okay, okay. So tell me. What's she like? Can I meet her?"

Two minutes ago I couldn't wait to tell him about Lark. Now I don't want to. I couldn't stand to have him talk about her as if she was just some girl. Just some girl to get it over with. Besides, where do I begin? How do I describe Lark? I don't have the words.

"Never mind."

"Come on, Bren. I didn't mean anything. Tell me."

I shake my head. "You don't get it."

He looks hurt. "How do you know?"

"I just do."

"That's not fair."

He's right. It's not fair. We've always trusted each other to understand. And we always have. But this is different. All of a sudden I don't want to share Lark with anyone. Not even Kesh.

"Forget it," I say.

Kesh gets up. "Man, you know what? I don't care if you're sick, you're really being an asshole."

He puts on his jacket and leaves.

I feel terrible. I know Kesh is right. I *am* being an asshole. But I don't care. There's only one thing on my mind. I can't wait to see Lark.

Chapter Thirteen

I hurry to her room. She's sleeping.

Standing in the doorway, staring at her, I'm shocked. She's even thinner. I know it's not possible that she actually lost that much weight overnight. It must just be that I'm seeing her with fresh eyes. The hollow under her collarbone is like a crater. Her cheek is sunken beneath the ridge of cheekbone. The wispy curls have fallen out again and her head is bald. Her skin is so pale that I almost think I can see the skeleton beneath.

I turn away, tears in my eyes. For the first time, I think the unthinkable. Then, immediately, No!

Blindly, I stagger into the hall. Harj catches me. "Hey, watch where you're going," she teases. Her smile disappears as she looks past me to see where I've come from. She pauses. "Brendan."

I dash away my tears. "Yeah?"

"Don't get too attached. Don't get your hopes up."

I throw her arms off. "Shut up! Don't say that!"

I run to my room, slam the door, throw myself on my bed.

It can't happen, I think. It can't.

A chill shudders through me. I feel more afraid than I've ever felt.

I have blood tests. Finally my counts are coming up. Slowly. Too slowly for me. But up. More healthy white blood cells. Red blood cells. Platelets.

Up.

Up.

Lark's cousin Annie, who is donating her bone marrow, has checked into the hospital. They're spending lots of time together, and I don't see much of Lark.

Annie is blond like Lark, only taller and more solid. She's a terrific person. She has a warm smile and she makes Lark laugh. She's nice to me when we meet and she tells me she's glad to hear that my treatment seems to be going well. She fetches lemon tea for me while she's fetching it for Lark. It's incredible of her to go through this for Lark, because donating bone marrow is painful and it can be dangerous for the donor.

I want Annie to go away. I'm jealous of her. I know it's stupid and petty and ridiculous of me, but I don't care. I want Lark to myself.

One evening I go to see Lark. She's finished with her chemo. Tomorrow she starts several days of radiation, the last blast before her bone-marrow transplant. From that point, she has to be in isolation because she'll be so defenseless. This is my last chance to see her before the operation.

She's in the middle of a riot of color, sitting on her turquoise bedspread, canopied by the purple scarves. She's wearing a red wooly sweater and a blue and gold tuque. Lottie, the yellow stuffed sheep, is on her lap.

Typical Lark.

"Hey," I say.

"Hey! Come sit."

I do. "How are you doing with…you know…what's coming?" I ask.

She smiles. "Good. Excited. Ready."

I can't believe how calm she is. I think I'm more nervous than she is.

She gives a little shiver and hugs herself.

"What's the matter?" I say.

"I'm fine, don't worry. Just cold." She shivers again. "I've been chilled all day."

No surprise, I think, considering she's skin and bones.

An idea hits. "Come with me," I say.

"Where to?"

"You'll see."

She grins. "I love surprises."

I wrap her in the bedspread and lead her down the hall to the hydrotherapy room. There's a deep tub in it, with jets. They use it to ease muscle aches from chemo. I've soaked in there when I've had the chills.

When Lark sees where we're going, she smiles. "Perfect." She stops and turns. "Be right back." She trails the bedspread like a royal robe.

While she's gone, I start filling the tub. She comes back with candles, which she sets around the ledge of the tub.

Humidity from the hot water starts filling the room.

When the tub is full, she lights the candles. I dim the lights. We stare at each other, then start to undress. It's the first time I've ever done this and not felt self-conscious. There's nothing sexy here, no seduction. It's just a boy and a girl getting naked.

She's even skinnier than she looks with clothes on. Her breasts are two tiny bumps. Her hip bones jut out. Her legs are sticks. She's beautiful.

She shivers again. I take her hand and we lower ourselves into the water. At first she sits clutching her knees to her chest, and I can tell she's still cold. But little by little she stretches out. Soon she's floating next to me.

We don't talk. There's everything to say, and nothing. We just float, fingertips touching, our bodies lit by candlelight that shimmers on the water.

When it's time to come out, I wrap Lark in a huge towel and rub her all over. I help her dress in all her layers.

We walk hand in hand back down the hall. Always before, Lark's taken care of me. Tonight I take charge. I tuck her in. I stroke her bare head until her eyelids droop.

Then I go back to my room.

For the first time in my life, I pray.

Chapter Fourteen

I'm feeling stronger. My blood counts are up. I haven't had another infection. In a few days I'll have another bone-marrow biopsy. If the cancer cells have come back, I'll have to have another cycle of chemo. If not, I'll be in remission and I can go home. I'm trying not to be too confident, but my doctor says it looks good.

Lark has her operation. All day I can hardly breathe. Every half hour I bug Harj for news.

She shakes her head. "Still in surgery."

"No news."

"Too soon."

Finally she rushes into my room. "She survived the operation!"

I leap off my bed and grab her in a hug.

The news is good. Lark's body isn't rejecting Annie's bone marrow. She's recovering. She's stabilizing.

But then, a few days later, Harj pushes past me in the hall, her face averted.

I grab her arm. Her face is lined, tense.

"What? *What?*"

"She has a low-grade fever."

Infection.

My insides clench. "Does that mean—?"

Harj shakes her head. "No need to panic. She's on antibiotics. They should do the trick."

I hear what she's not saying. I don't let myself go there.

The infection gets worse. They double the antibiotics.

Lark rallies a little.

I hold my breath.

"Congratulations, Brendan," says my oncologist. "Your biopsy results are excellent. You're in remission."

My mom grabs me in a hug. My dad bursts out crying, then laughs, then cries again.

"Whoo!" A jolt of joy runs through me. For the first time since I heard the word *leukemia*, I feel a weight lift off me. The bands that have been cinched around my chest loosen, and I breathe deeply.

Remission. No cancer. I have a chance. I'm not *cured*—no one's using that word, and no one will for a long time. I'll have more treatments over the next nine months and then, if all is well, go on pills. I've got a long way to go. But I've made it through this round. For the first time I allow myself to think, *I'm going to live.*

I go back to the ward with my parents. I have to pack up, get instructions, make appointments for more tests.

I go to my room and start collecting my things. My clothes, which are now loose on me. My schoolbooks, which I've scarcely opened. My basketball picture, a few novels, my music. My collection of baseball caps and tuques. I'll still need those for a while.

I move more and more slowly as I pack. I know I'm dragging my feet. I don't want to leave without seeing Lark, without knowing she's going to be okay. Besides, I need to find out how to get in touch with her outside the hospital. Because I'm definitely going to do that. We'll hang out. We'll tease each other about our wispy hair growing in, and I'll take her to a basketball game and we'll dance and eat pudding and listen to music.

My parents come in. They've done the paperwork, and they're all smiles. They look like they've dropped ten years each. They're anxious to get home, call everybody they know, celebrate.

"I can't go yet," I tell them.

"What? Why not?"

"I have to find out about Lark."

"But, Brendan—"

"I have to."

They exchange a look.

"I'm not going until I've seen her—"

Just then, outside my door, I hear, "Oh no."

I rush out. Harj has her hands over her face. I pull them away. Tears roll down her cheeks.

"Harj—what—? Please—no—"

She shakes her head.

"No!"

Harj puts her arms around me. "The infection got out of control. She didn't make it," she whispers, choking back sobs.

I throw off her arms, stare at her. "No! No—you're lying—It can't—no!"

"Brendan—"

I turn and run back to my room, past my parents, who are standing in the hall. I start throwing things. The stuff I've gathered. Books. Clothes. Shoes. Pillows. Blankets. They hit the walls, scatter on the floor.

My parents rush in. "Brendan, no," my mom says.

My dad tries to grab my arms.

I throw him off.

"Brendan, please, get ahold of yourself. This isn't good for you. Let's go home. We'll—"

"Leave me alone. I'm not coming." I heave a book at the wall.

"Brendan—," my dad begins.

My mom cuts him off. "He needs some space," I hear her whisper. She puts a hand on my arm. "We'll wait for you in the car."

They leave.

Chapter Fifteen

There's nothing left to throw. I pace back and forth.

It can't be. It can't.

I pound my fist on the wall. It hurts. I enjoy the pain.

She can't be gone.

The inside of my head roars. I want to kill someone. I want to murder God. I want to hurt myself.

I can't go on without her.

Something cracks. I throw myself on the bed and howl. A sound comes out of me, like an animal roaring in pain. The sobs rip up from the pit of my stomach.

I draw my knees up and curl into a ball. I feel a hand on my back, gentle and warm, and know it's Harj. I hear her sobs. I lean into her hand.

She strokes me. I grunt and cry.

After a while I feel her get up. I hear her move around the room, picking up my things, putting them in a bag.

Finally my tears are spent. I lie there in a heap.

Harj comes back. She sits down beside me again. "It's hard. Believe me, I know, Brendan."

I have no answer for this. I don't say anything.

Harj leans over and gives me a kiss on the cheek. "You take care of yourself,

Brendan," she whispers. "Stay strong. Stay healthy. I'll see you in a couple of months."

She leaves.

I lie there for a minute, then force myself to get up. I take one last look around my room. It looks empty now, a stranger's room. I pick up my bag and trudge down the hall.

On my way out, I go into Lark's room. Her stuff is still in it. The purple canopy. The turquoise bedspread. The sunflowers, the peacock's feather. The picture of the ballerina, the chocolate-smeared children. Lottie the sheep.

Lark is so present. I can see her. Smell her. Feel her.

It can't be.

The anger returns. Screw this. Screw everything.

I grab Lottie from the bed, crush her to me as if I want to crush the stuffing out of her.

"Why?" I wail into Lottie's wool. I don't know who, or what, I'm asking the question of. I just know there's no answer.

I sit down, under the canopy, clutching Lottie. I see Lark, fluttering her arms, that day she told me about "The Dying Swan." I remember when she showed me how to lie on the floor to fight the nausea. Her delight in the taste of chocolate, of butterscotch. When we danced. *I got a little red rooster too lazy to crow for day*...How we floated in the candlelight.

Was that only a few nights ago?

I remember our fights. When she insisted it was *so* worth it to make her room beautiful. When she laughed at me for calling her a saint. When she gave me crap for being rude to my relatives.

Her words come back to me. *It's about how you want to live, with whatever time you've got.*

How *do* I want to live?

I know what Lark would say. You live like you dance. Like you play basketball. Like you taste butterscotch pudding.

But I can't, I think. Not without her.

Then I hear her voice again. *You take the next breath, and the next. That's brave.*

I don't feel brave. I don't feel anything except furious and empty.

But what else can I do?

I place Lottie back on the pillow. Tuck her in. Then I pull down one of the purple scarves. Her parents won't mind. It's just one. I crush it to my face. It smells of the lemon tea she always drank. It smells of her peppermint shampoo. I stuff it in my bag.

I close the door behind me.

I turn and go, down the hall, down the elevator. I step outside. Sunshine falls on my face. I pause, letting it soak in.

Over my bald head I tug the baseball cap my teammates gave me.

I hear the hum of traffic, the *brrring* of a bicycle bell, a kid's shout of laughter from the park across the street.

I walk toward my parents' waiting car, taking deep breaths, filling my lungs with air.

Acknowledgments

The author would like to thank Sandra Diersch, James and Lynn Hill, Corinne and Dave Roth, Merri Schwartz, Amy Schwartz, Bill Schwartz and Stephen Capon.

Titles in the Series

orca soundings

orca soundings

For more information on all the books
in the Orca Soundings series, please visit
www.orcabook.com.